BEAR NEEDS HELP!

D0068391

Written by Rita Schlachter
Illustrated by Patti Boyd

Troll Associates

Library of Congress Cataloging in Publication Data

Schlachter, Rita.
  Bear needs help!

  Summary: Rabbit proves you don't have to be big to
help when his friend Bear gets a bee in his ear.
  [1. Size—Fiction. 2. Rabbits—Fiction. 3. Bears—
Fiction] I. Boyd, Patti, ill. II. Title.
PZ7.S34657Be   1986   [E]   85-14052
ISBN 0-8167-0600-X (lib. bdg.)
ISBN 0-8167-0601-8 (pbk.)

BEAR
NEEDS HELP!

Rabbit knocked on Bear's front
door.

"Come in," said Bear.
He was in bed.
"I heard you were not feeling
well," said Rabbit.

6

"It's my ear," said Bear. "I went
looking for some honey. I put my
paw inside the tree. A bee flew
out. He flew in my ear, and he's
still there buzzing around."

"I will take care of you," said
Rabbit.
"You can't take care of me," said
Bear. "You're too small."

"I don't have to be big to take care of you," said Rabbit. "I will make you a bowl of instant chicken-noodle soup for lunch."

"You can't even reach my table,"
said Bear.
"I can stand on a chair," said
Rabbit. "Now I can reach the
table. I think a hot lunch will
make you feel better."

10

"A hot lunch will not make me feel better. Getting this bee out of my ear will make me feel better," said Bear.

"Hot soup will help you feel better. Then we can think of a way to get the bee out of your ear," said Rabbit.

"But you can't read. So how can
you fix my lunch?" asked Bear.

"I can find the soup in the
cupboard," said Rabbit. "You
can read the directions to me."
Rabbit took the box of soup from
the cupboard.

"You need a small pan to put the soup in," Bear read. "You have to add two cups of water to the dry soup."

Rabbit got a measuring cup so he would know when he had two cups of water.

"The number 2 is on the cup,"
said Rabbit. "I can read numbers
and letters, but I can't read
words."

"This will not work," said Bear. "You have to boil the water to make the soup hot. You are too small to use the stove. Now I can't have any lunch, and I won't feel better."

"You'll get lunch," said Rabbit.
"I'll put the chair by the sink. I'll
let the water get very hot. Then
I will put two cups of hot water
into the pan with the soup."

Rabbit stirred the hot water and dry soup together in the pan. He poured the soup into a big bowl. It smelled good.

Bear sat up in bed. "This is good," said Bear. "It's not too hot. When I boil the soup on the stove it's too hot to eat. I always have to wait till it cools. The hot water from the sink is just right."

After lunch, Bear tried to rest,
but the bee in his ear did not
want to rest.

The bee buzzed louder and
louder. Bear jumped out of bed.
He hopped on his right foot. He
hit the right side of his head with
his big paw.

"I can't stand this any longer,"
said Bear.
He hopped around the room,
first on one foot, then on the
other. Bear was so big the dishes
started to rattle in the cupboard.

The light hanging from the
ceiling began swinging from side
to side. The flower pot went
thump, thump, thump to the
other side of the windowsill.

"The soup did not help my ear,"
said Bear.
He changed feet. Now he was
hopping on his left foot.

BUZZZZzz

"Stop! Stop!" said Rabbit.
Bear did not stop.
"I'll think of a way to help," said
Rabbit.
"You can't help me," said Bear.

BUZZZZZzz

"Jumping around won't help
your ear," said Rabbit. "Sit
down and be quiet."

31

Bear sat down, but he was not
still. He put his right leg over his
left leg. Then he put his left leg
over his right leg. He rubbed his
ear.

"Come on. Let's think hard.
What do bees like?" asked
Rabbit.
"Me!" said Bear.

"No," said Rabbit. "If it is a bee,
what is he looking for?"

"Honey," said Bear. "But I'm not going to let you put honey in my ear."

"No," said Rabbit. "I guess that would be too sticky. Let's think some more. What do insects fly to?"

"Food," said Bear. "But you're
not going to put food in my ear
either. Hurry! Think of something
else bees like."
And Bear began to rub his ear
again.

"Bees like other bees," said
Rabbit.

"No! No!" said Bear, jumping
out of the chair. "The bee in my
ear may not fly out, but the
other bee may fly in. I don't
need two bees in my ear."

BUZzzzᶻᶻᶻᶻᶻᶻᶻᶻᶻ

"I have it," said Rabbit. "Bees like flowers. They gather nectar from flowers."

Rabbit pulled a flower out of the
flowerpot. He held the flower
close to Bear's ear. They waited
and waited.

"Maybe he doesn't like yellow
flowers," grumbled Bear.
"Be patient," said Rabbit. "Let's
try a little longer."

Suddenly, Bear heard a *pop* in his ear. He heard buzzing, but the buzzing was not in his ear anymore. The bee was flying around the room. He flew this way and that way. Then he flew out the window.

Bear rubbed his ear.
"You're right," said Bear. "You
don't have to be big to help. You
just have to stop and think.
Thank you, Rabbit."

And the two friends hurried
outside to play.